W9-ALW-158

ADDY-MATIC

and the TOASTERRIFIC!

To my Adeline,
May you never stop creating.

Be sure to visit **Addy-matic.com** for some fun
machine ideas you can build at home!
You'll also learn more about the *real* Addy-matic
and be the first to know about
the next books in the series:

Addy-matic and the Swingamajig
Addy-matic and the Critter Gitter

Copyright © 2017 by Curtis Mark Williams, Edition 001

All rights reserved. No part of this book may be reproduced without written permission.

ISBN-13: 978-1981970988, ISBN-10: 1981970983

ADDY-MATIC

and the TOASTERRIFIC!

by
Curtis Mark Williams

Illustrated by
Pascale Lafond

7:00am! The buzzer blared.
"Harumph!" a sleepy voice declared.
She hit the snooze, "Morning stinks."
And snuggled in for ten more winks.

Her real name was Adeline
But like she told a friend of mine,
"Call me Addy" then a warning:
"Just don't call me in the morning."

Groggily and unawares
She grudged awake and trudged downstairs,
With hair awry and belly grumblin'
Toward the toaster she went stumblin'.

"Ugh – I'm never in the mood
When I wake to make some food."

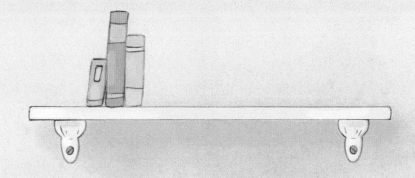

"I wish that while I'm still in bed
My food could make itself instead!"

Then it happened. Addy froze.
And in her mind a thought arose.
"Wait a sec – perhaps it can..."
She mused and smirked and hatched a plan.

Here is what she did intend:
"Working backwards from the end,
I'll find a way to automate
Getting toast made on a plate!"

But 'automate' did not quite fit
So Addy tweaked it just a bit...

"Instead of something *auto*-matic
This thing will be *Addy*-matic!"

Starting off, she did decide
To turn the toaster on its side.
"That's how I will get my wish,
The toast will pop onto the dish!"

"Now, how to pull the toaster lever?
I'll need something really clever...
A mousetrap and a piece of string
Placed just right, could be the thing!"

"To spring the trap I'll need a mouse,
But there aren't any in our house...wait!
My cat, Ruby, has a toy.
I'll use that one in my ploy!"

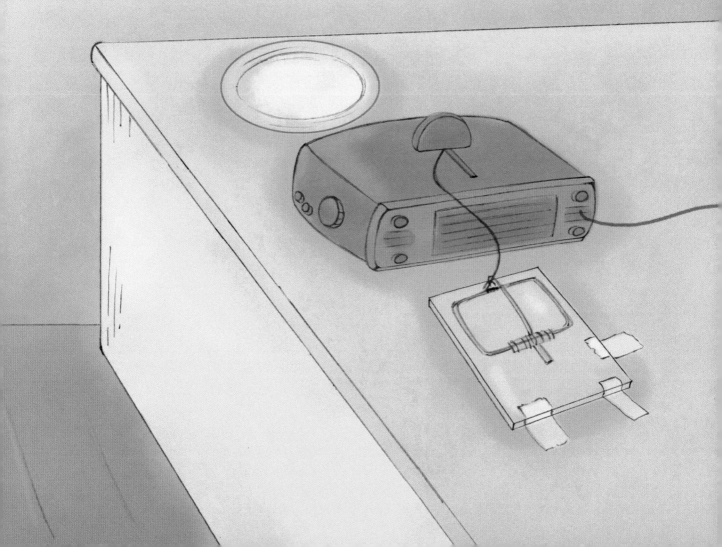

"To push the mouse in? Let me think...
A broom might be the missing link!
And then to give the broom a whack
I'll roll a melon down a track!"

"I'll start the track high on a shelf
The melon cannot roll itself...?
I'll knock it with a frying pan
Duct-taped to the ceiling fan!"

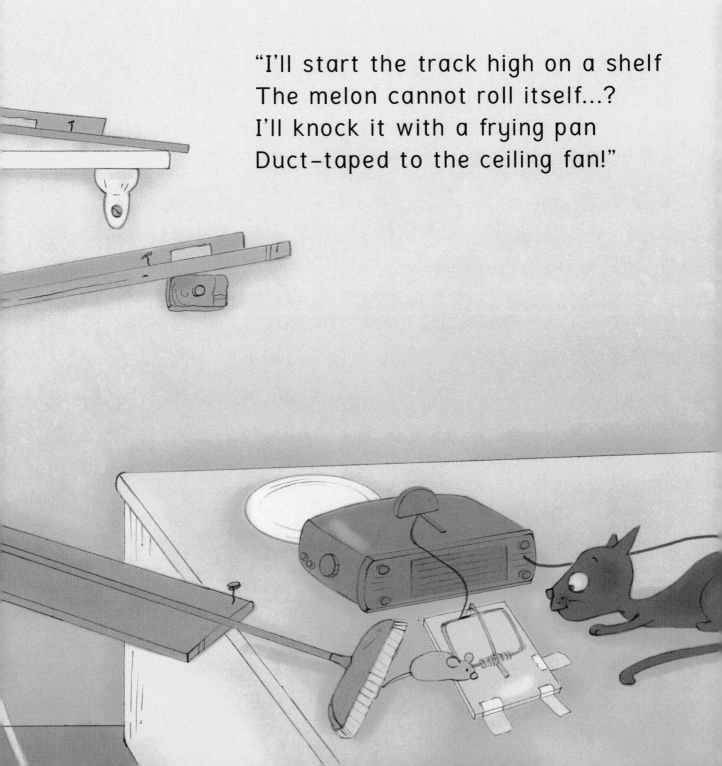

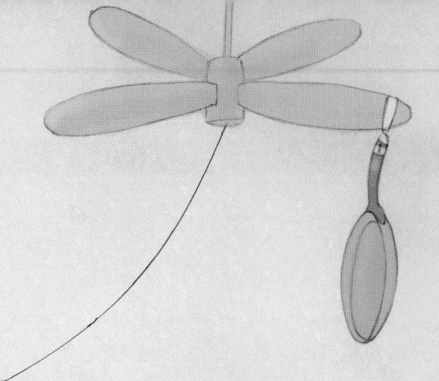

"Now, how to start the ceiling fan?
My sister's hamster, Hammy, can!
He can run inside his wheel
And wind the chain like a fishing reel."

"To make him run I'll need a peach
To land just inches out of reach
(Hammy sometimes can be lazy
His favorite fruit will drive him crazy)."

"To get a peach won't be that hard
I have a peach tree in my yard.
The hard part is to get it in, though...
I'll fling it through an open window!"

"The peach can fall into a bucket
On the seesaw – that could huck it!"
Now she faced quite a feat:
What to drop on the other seat?

"Something heavy? I'll use the ladder!
How it tips is another matter...
The garage door lifting, that should do it!"
She placed the ladder right next to it.

"Beneath the seesaw I will lay
The garage door clicker in the way.
So when the peach falls in the pail
The weight will click it without fail."

"To get that peach out of the tree
I'll need some shears to set it free.
To squeeze the shears and make 'em cut,
The clothesline rope can pull them shut!"

"I need to drop it from a height...
My bedroom window seems just right!
I'll rest it on my window ledge
Precariously on the edge."

"And then, to drop it right on cue,
I think I'll need to fix it to..."

"...A big balloon which I'll hold still
Between the window and the sill."

"And when it pops that bird will fly!
Now how to pop it? What to try?
A pin? A tack? A power saw?
Wait, I know! A kitty's claw!"

Near the window on a chair
She laid dear Ruby sleeping there.
"When my clock rings there's no doubt
She'll spring straight up
with all claws out!"

"WHEW!"

And that was that.
Addy smiled, admiring her creation.
No more waiting, no more work. Perfect automation.
All it needed was a name, something scientific...

"I christen thee", she said with glee,
the effortless...TOASTERRIFIC!"

The sun went down, she washed and brushed
And headed off to bed,
With dreams of automatic toast
Still dancing in her head.

Morning sunrise came at last, a new day had begun,
The clock ticked down the seconds, then 5-4-3-2-1...

7:00am!
The alarm bell rang!
Addy stirred,
Ruby sprang!

The balloon went pop!
The turkey dropped!
The shears went snip!
The peach ker-plopped!

YAWN!

The clicker clicked!
The garage door
knocked!
The ladder tipped!
The seesaw rocked!

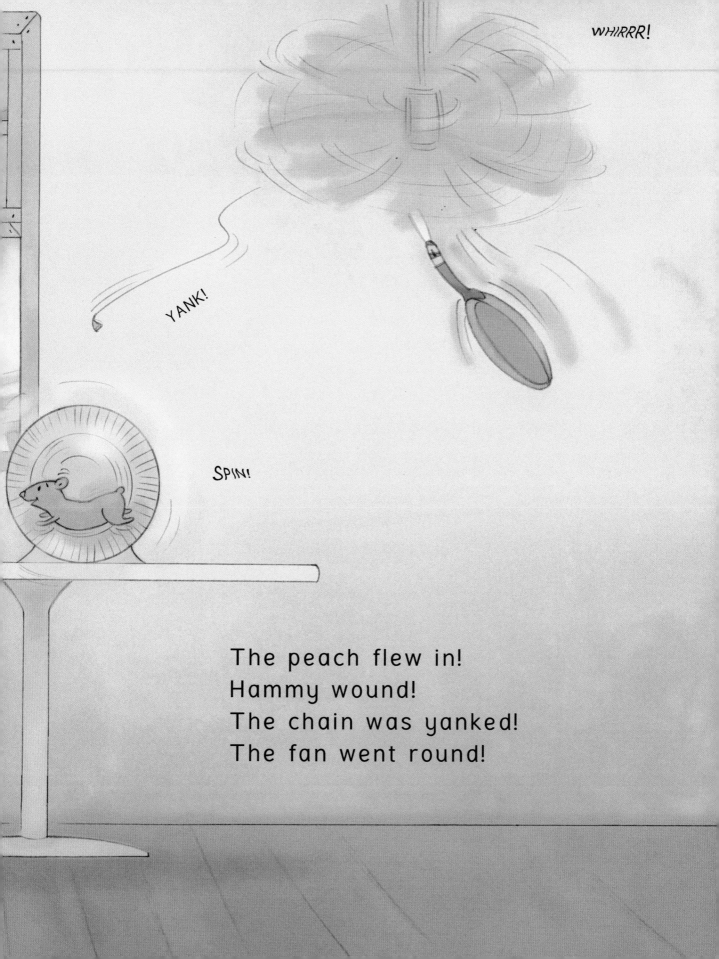

The peach flew in!
Hammy wound!
The chain was yanked!
The fan went round!

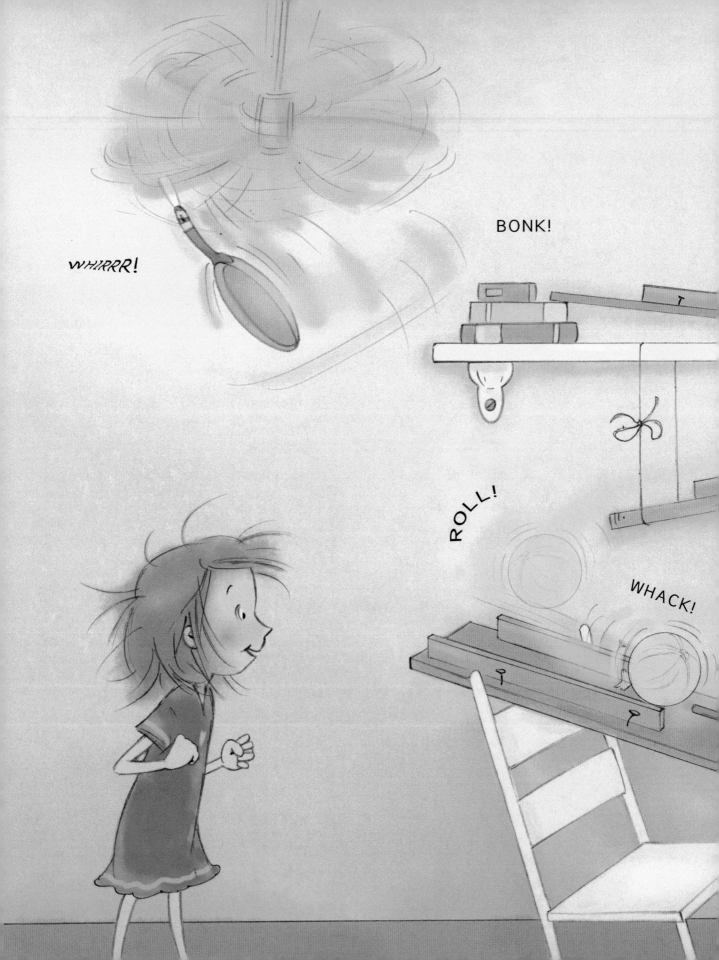

The melon rolled!
The broom got pushed!
The trap got snapped!
The mouse got smushed!

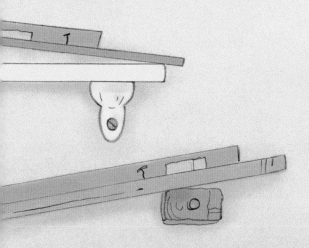

The string pulled!
The lever dropped!
The toaster warmed!
Everything stopped.

A second later, the toaster...POPPED!

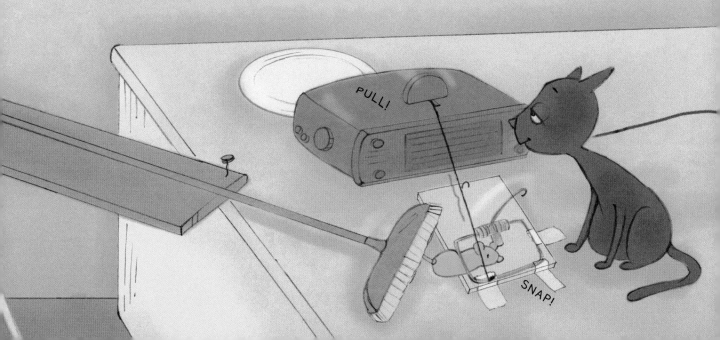

Addy stared...
Then smacked her head!

"Oh my gosh, I FORGOT THE BREAD!"

Glossary
(in order of appearance)

Blared - Made a loud sound

Harumph - An expression of protest

Declared - Announced something

Snuggled - Moved oneself into a cozy position

Wink - A brief period of sleep

Groggily - In a slow or weakened manner caused by sleepiness

Grudged - Grumbled, complained; was dissatisfied

Trudged - Walked wearily with heavy, slow steps

Awry - Turned or twisted, crooked, out of place

Arose - Sprang up; came into being

Mused - Thought about; meditated on

Smirked - Smiled in a self-satisfied kind of way

Hatched - Used one's brain to plan or design

Intend - To fix the mind upon something to be accomplished

Automate - To replace human effort with a machine

Tweaked - Adjusted; fine-tuned

Ploy - A plan of action to accomplish a specific goal

Duct Tape - Generally gray adhesive tape used for many purposes

Huck - To throw a long way

Feat - A rare or difficult accomplishment

Liberate - To set free, as from imprisonment

Counterweight - A heavy object mechanically linked to another object which helps it to be raised or lowered

Precariously - In an insecure or unstable manner

Christen - To name

Glossary - a list of words relating to a specific text with explanations; a brief dictionary

Made in the USA
Monee, IL
15 December 2020

53641006R00021